When God Created My Toes

Dandi Daley Mackall
illustrated by David Hohn

WATERBROOK
PRESS

WHEN GOD CREATED MY TOES
PUBLISHED BY WATERBROOK PRESS
12265 Oracle Boulevard, Suite 200
Colorado Springs, Colorado 80921
A division of Random House Inc.

ISBN 978-1-4000-7315-3

Published in the United States by WaterBrook Multnomah, an imprint of The Doubleday Publishing Group, a division of Random House Inc., New York.

WATERBROOK and its deer colophon are registered trademarks of Random House Inc.

The Cataloging-in-Publication Data is on file with the Library of Congress.

Printed in the United States of a America
2008—First Edition

10 9 8 7 6 5 4 3 2 1

For you created my inmost being;
    you knit me together in my
        mother's womb.
I praise you because I am fearfully
    and wonderfully made;
    your works are wonderful,
    I know that full well.

— Psalm 139:13–16

When God
created
my toes

Did he make them wiggle?

Did he know I'd giggle?

Did he have to hold his nose
when God created my toes?

When God
created
my knees

Did he put bones in 'em?

Did he know I'd skin 'em?

Did we sing our ABCs
when God created my knees?

When God created my hip,

Did I hear him say,

"Hip, hip, hooray!"?

Did we do a double flip
when God created my hip?

When God
created
my hands

Did my fingers snap?

Did he help me clap?

Did we cheer for angel bands
when God created my hands?

When God
created
my head

Did he know my hair

Would look fine up there?

How I wonder what we said
when God created my head!

When God
created
my eyes

Could I see him too,

Playing peek-a-boo?

Did we hide in cloudy skies
when God created my eyes?

When God
created
my nose

Did he know I'd sneeze

In a wintry breeze?

Did we kiss like Eskimos
when God created my nose?

When God created my heart

Did he make it beat?

Did he make it sweet?

Did I love him from the start
when God created my heart?

When God
created
me